THE
BEAR
IN MY
FAMILY

Maya Tatsukawa

WATCH OUT!

Dial Books
for Young Readers

To my parents and those who have been there for me like family, bear or not

Dial Books for Young Readers
An imprint of Penguin Random House LLC, New York

Copyright © 2020 by Maya Tatsukawa

Library of Congress Cataloging-in-Publication Data
Names: Tatsukawa, Maya, author, illustrator. | Title: The bear in my family / Maya Tatsukawa.
Description: New York : Dial Books for Young Readers, [2019] | Summary: "It's not easy living with a bear, but one little boy learns that sometimes, a bear in the family can end up to be the best thing in the world"—Provided by publisher.
Identifiers: LCCN 2019021274 (print) | LCCN 2019022311 (ebook) | ISBN 9780525555827 (hardcover)
Subjects: CYAC: Bears—Fiction. | Family life—Fiction.
Classification: LCC PZ7.1.T38375 Be 2019 (print) | LCC PZ7.1.T38375 (ebook) | DDC [E]—dc23

Printed in China
1 3 5 7 9 10 8 6 4 2

Design by Mina Chung • Text set in Mikado
This art was created digitally with handmade textures.

I live with a bear.

The bear sleeps

there.

This is what the bear
looks like.

big ears
mean eyes
sharp teeth
strong arms
short but quick legs

The bear is really **loud,**

really **bossy,**

and always hungry.

Maybe too strong.

For some reason, my parents
think the bear is family.

I try to tell my mom the truth.

I wonder why my parents
don't see what I see.

I guess a **loud** bear isn't so bad.

Or a **strong** bear, either.

Even a **hungry** bear can come in handy.

And a **fast** bear
makes me fast, too.

Best of all is a bear
that looks out for me.

And who doesn't love . . .

I TOLD YOU

Because what's better than one bear?
TWO!